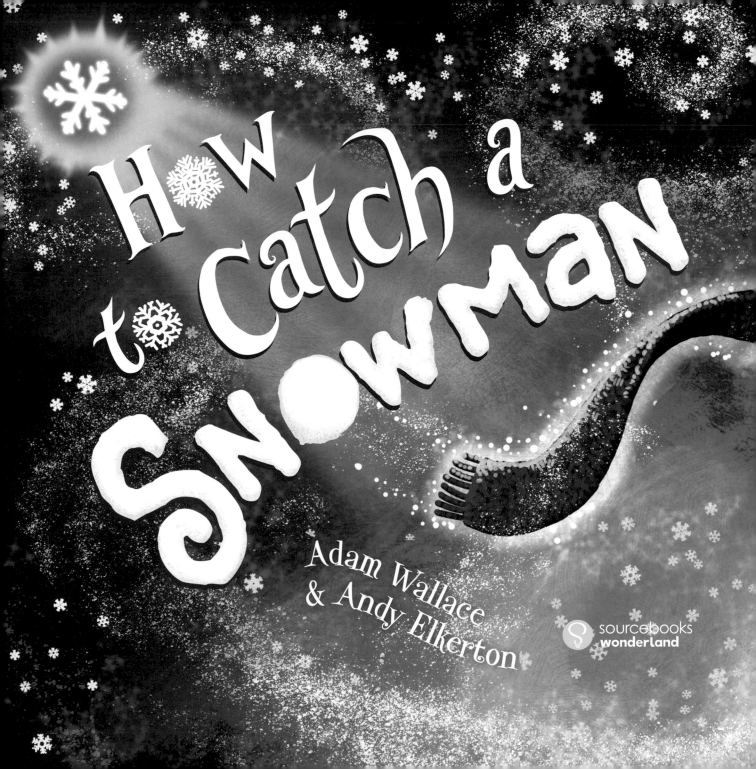

When the moon is full on a snowy night,
something **magical** happens if the time is right.

LIBRARY

Do You Want to Build a Snowman?

GRAND PRIZE

It's not an old silk hat that brings me to life,
but the enchanted **SNOW STAR** shining down at midnight.

I don't **thumpity-thump** or give warm hugs—
that's for my friends to do.

These clever kids will try to trap me,
but who will catch me...you?

That first trap was a good attempt,
your running made me SMILE.

Your net of scarves might've done the trick,
but it's left you all in a pile!

Now this trap is an improvement
and my escape is no guarantee.
But I'll skate fast and with a spin
you're covered in snow like me.

A snowman who loves summer?

I've heard of this before.

What you didn't know is I can fly!
Stand back and watch me SOAR.

Chasing me down the hillside,
you're really good at skiing!
But when I **bounce** into a snowball,
I'm really good at fleeing!

I have to admit, that trap you made
was a clever use of snow.

A snowman shop! That's quite a treat,
made *special* just for me!
Perhaps I'll grab a hat or scarf,
or maybe two or three.

Snowman
Accessories

You built me with a carrot nose–
I think that's kind of cute.
But cuter still is trying to catch me
with vegetables and fruit!

This **WINTER WONDERLAND** is great—
so bright and full of fun!
But snow globes can't hold me for long.
Too bad—I've gotta run!

SNOWGLOBE 9000

Glue

Woo-hoo! Your sleigh ride sure is fun–
I love gliding down this slide!
But I think I'll skip the trampoline
that ends this jolly joy ride.

Now that was one fantastic trap
and very well thought through.
Nice try! Well done! Magnificent job!
But I'll still escape from you!

Once I've **ESCAPED** your final trap,
you get called in for dinner.
As the sun sets, it seems to me,
that I am the contest winner.

You tried so hard to *catch* me,
I'm glad I'm free, it's true.
But perhaps before I'm on my way,
I can leave a gift for you.

Copyright © 2018, 2020 by Sourcebooks
Text by Adam Wallace
Illustrations by Andy Elkerton
Cover and internal design © 2018, 2020 by Sourcebooks

Sourcebooks and the colophon are registered trademarks of Sourcebooks.

All rights reserved.

The art was first sketched, then painted digitally with brushes designed by the artist.

Published by Sourcebooks Wonderland, an imprint of Sourcebooks Kids
P.O. Box 4410, Naperville, Illinois 60567-4410
(630) 961-3900
sourcebookskids.com

Library of Congress Cataloging-in-Publication Data is on file with the publisher.

Source of Production: Wing King Tong Paper Products Co. Ltd., Shenzhen,
Guangdong Province, China
Date of Production: April 2021
Run Number: 5021905

Printed and bound in China.
WKT 10 9 8 7 6 5 4 3